Loud
Daniel O'Dowd

written by
Julie Fulton

illustrated by
Elina Ellis

Daniel O'Dowd was ever so loud.

He shouted wherever he went.

At the zoo the chimps cried when his mouth opened wide
and the elephant hid in a tent.

When he shouted at school, his teacher, Miss Pool,
wrapped a **big** woolly scarf round her head.
She declared, "I've no doubt, if you **stopped** shouting ou
you would hear something useful instead."

The class went to visit Professor McWhizzit.
He built things like airports for bees,
mad machines to cut hair, an invisible chair
and a telescope made out of cheese.

OPEN DAY!

INVISIBLE
CHAIR

Daniel shouted, "Yippee! Let me look, let me see!"
All the noise made Miss Pool start to frown.
Daniel's shouts grew so loud they scared all the crowd
and made the town's lighthouse fall down.

Daniel screwed up his face and looked up into space.

He saw satellites, planets and stars.

Then he shouted in shock, "I can see a huge rock and it's racing towards us from Mars!"

Professor McWhizzit said, "Hang on a minute!
I've a rocket I made from a clock.
If I send Daniel out and he gives a big shout,
I think he could shatter the rock!"

Daniel clambered on board, the engines all roared
and the rocket shot way, way up high.
It zoomed past the moon and a spaceship and soon
it was next to the rock in the sky.

Daniel gave a loud shout, the noise echoed about,
but the rock simply **shuddered** and **twitched**.
So he shouted lots more, more than ever before,
and.........

BANG!

the rock burst into bits.

The Professor said, "Wow! You can stop shouting now. I'll explain how to fly back to Earth."

But the boy didn't hear what was said in his ear -
he was **cheering** for all he was worth.

The rocket sped on and soon it had gone
many miles from young Daniel's home town.
When he saw with a fright the earth vanish from sight
Daniel cried out, "I want to get down!"

He bellowed and yowled, he hollered and howled,
'til his face went a bright rosy red.
Then he thought of Miss Pool and her listening rule.
"I mustn't shout, I must listen instead."

The Professor cried, "Quick! Pull the red control stick."
Daniel pulled it as hard as he could.
The rocket swung round and flew back to the ground,
landing right where the lighthouse had stood.

Daniel O'Dowd was no longer so loud.

His adventure had made it quite plain.

"I will **listen** lots more, I won't shout like before...

...unless Earth needs saving again!"

The End

Loud Daniel O'Dowd

An original concept by Julie Fulton

© Julie Fulton

Written by Julie Fulton

Illustrated by Elina Ellis

Published by MAVERICK ARTS PUBLISHING LTD

Studio 3A, City Business Centre, 6 Brighton Road,

Horsham, West Sussex, RH13 5BB

+44 (0)1403 256941

© Maverick Arts Publishing Limited

Published March 2016

A CIP catalogue record for this book is available at the British Library.

ISBN 978-1-84886-200-5

www.maverickbooks.co.uk